Animal Travellers

Alan Trussell-Cullen

Australia • Brazil • Japan • Korea • Mexico • Singapore • Spain • United Kingdom • United States

Animal Travellers

Fast Forward
Turquoise Level 18

Text: Alan Trussell-Cullen
Editor: Johanna Rohan
Design: Stella Vassiliou
Series design: James Lowe
Production controller: Seona Galbally
Photo research: Michelle Cottrill
Audio recordings: Juliet Hill, Picture Start
Spoken by: Matthew King and Abbe Holmes

Acknowledgements
The author and publisher would like to acknowledge permission to reproduce material from the following sources: Photographs by AGE Fotostock/Steve Kaufman, pp 8-9; Auscape/Densey Cline, p15/Kathie Atkinson, p16 top; Bruce Coleman USA/Mark Newman, p20 top/Phillip Colla, p22 bottom; Corbis/Kennan Ward, p19 top/George H H Huey, p18 bottom/Steve Kaufman, p21 bottom; Getty Images/National Geographic, p21 top/Taxi, p18 top; istockphoto.com, pp 8 bottom, 12 right, 13 top/Eliza Snow, p17/Robert Hambley, p6; Photolibrary/Alamy/Keith Dannemiller, p12 left Alastair Shay, front cover bottom, back cover (butterfly), pp 1 bottom, 11 top/Animals Animals/Eastcott/Momatiuk, pp 20 bottom, 22 top/Stefano Nicolini, p13 bottom/Bill Bachman, pp 18-19/Bob Peterson, p10 top/Brenda Tharp, cover wrap/Chris Sharp, p7/Dan Guravich, p9/Eastcott/Momatiuk, p23/Erickson Production, p10 bottom/Jim Stimson, p11 bottom/Jim Watt, p4 bottom/ Peter Arnold/Ed Reschke, back cover, p16 bottom left/Ron Giling, p14/Peter Hawkey, pp 4 top, 5 top left/Photo Researchers, back cover (cocoon), p16 bottom right/Susan Seubert, p8 top/WK Fletcher, p5 top right/Yvette Cardozo, pp 4-5 centre; Photos.com, front cover top, pp 1 top, 3.

ISBN 978 0 17 012638 0
ISBN 978 0 17 012633 5 (set)

Cengage Learning Australia
Level 7, 80 Dorcas Street
South Melbourne, Victoria Australia 3205
Phone: 1300 790 853

Cengage Learning New Zealand
Unit 4B Rosedale Office Park
331 Rosedale Road, Albany, North Shore NZ 0632
Phone: 0508 635 766

For learning solutions, visit cengage.com.au

Printed in Australia by Ligare Pty Ltd
5 6 7 8 9 10 11 21 20 19 18 17

Evaluated in independent research by staff from the Department of Language, Literacy and Arts Education at the University of Melbourne.

Animal Travellers

Alan Trussell-Cullen

Contents

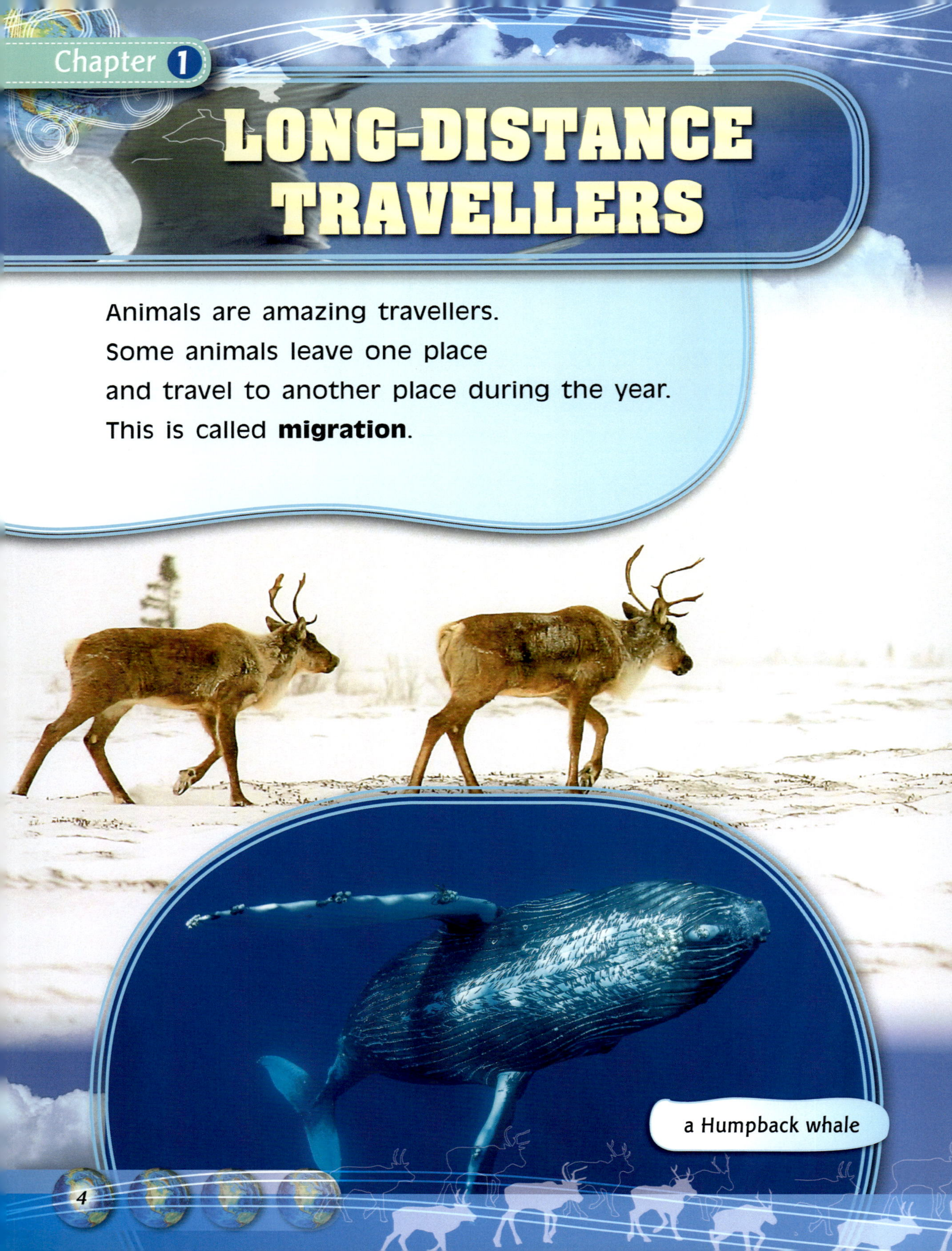

Chapter 1

LONG-DISTANCE TRAVELLERS

Animals are amazing travellers.
Some animals leave one place
and travel to another place during the year.
This is called **migration**.

a Humpback whale

There are many reasons why animals migrate – for food, warmth, or a safe place to **breed**.

There are many ways in which animals migrate – some fly, some swim and some walk.

Chapter 2

MONARCH BUTTERFLIES

Monarch butterflies are one of the most amazing animal travellers.

They make two huge journeys each year – one in autumn and one in spring.

Scientists think Monarch butterflies migrate to find **milkweed**.

The butterflies need milkweed to breed.

Scientists also think that Monarch butterflies migrate to get away from the cold weather.

In Canada and the northern parts of America, thousands of Monarch butterflies migrate in autumn.
This is their first journey.

Some Monarch butterflies fly to California, where they stay for the winter. About 300 million Monarch butterflies spend the winter in Mexico.

On their journey south, Monarch butterflies eat nectar from flowers, which gives them strength for their long journey.

Monarch butterflies face many dangers when they migrate.
Many butterflies are eaten by birds, some butterflies are killed by cars when flying across highways, and others are killed in storms.

Also, Monarch butterflies can't fly in a straight line because they have to fly around mountains and fight against strong winds.

Thousands of people help to track the migration of Monarch butterflies. Monarch butterfly watchers have found out some amazing facts about these butterflies.

Monarch butterflies may travel over 3200 kilometres on their journey.
They travel about 50 kilometres a day, at speeds of about 12 kilometres per hour.

The Monarch butterflies' second journey is in spring. The butterflies fly north.

On the way back north, the butterflies lay their eggs on milkweed, and then they die.
So, the butterflies that set out on this journey don't finish it.

The butterflies' eggs hatch into caterpillars
and feed on milkweed.
Soon, they turn into butterflies and set out to travel north.

an egg hatching

a Monarch caterpillar

a new Monarch butterfly

But, this generation of Monarch butterflies may not make it either.

Sometimes, it can take three or four generations of butterflies to make it back to Canada and North America.

Chapter 3

NORTHERN FUR SEALS

Northern fur seals spend winter in the warm waters near California.
There is lots of food for the seals,
but there are also lots of **predators**.

When spring comes, the Northern fur seals set out on a long journey to islands near Alaska.
These islands are a safe place for the seals to breed, as there are not as many predators.

The male seals arrive at the islands first. They fight for the best places to breed and wait for the females to arrive.

The females arrive about four weeks later. They each give birth to one seal pup.

male Northern fur seals fighting

a female Northern fur seal

a Northern fur seal pup and its mother

Northern fur seal pups

In the next few days, the seals mate again. When they return to the islands, one year later, the females will give birth to next year's seal pups.

After three months, the females and the young seals set off back to the warm waters off the coast of California.
Soon after, the males also leave the islands.

The fur seals travel 10 000 kilometres on their journey from California to Alaska and back again.

Glossary

breed to mate and produce offspring

migration to move from one place to another according to the seasons

milkweed an American plant with milky sap

predators animals that attack and eat other animals

Index